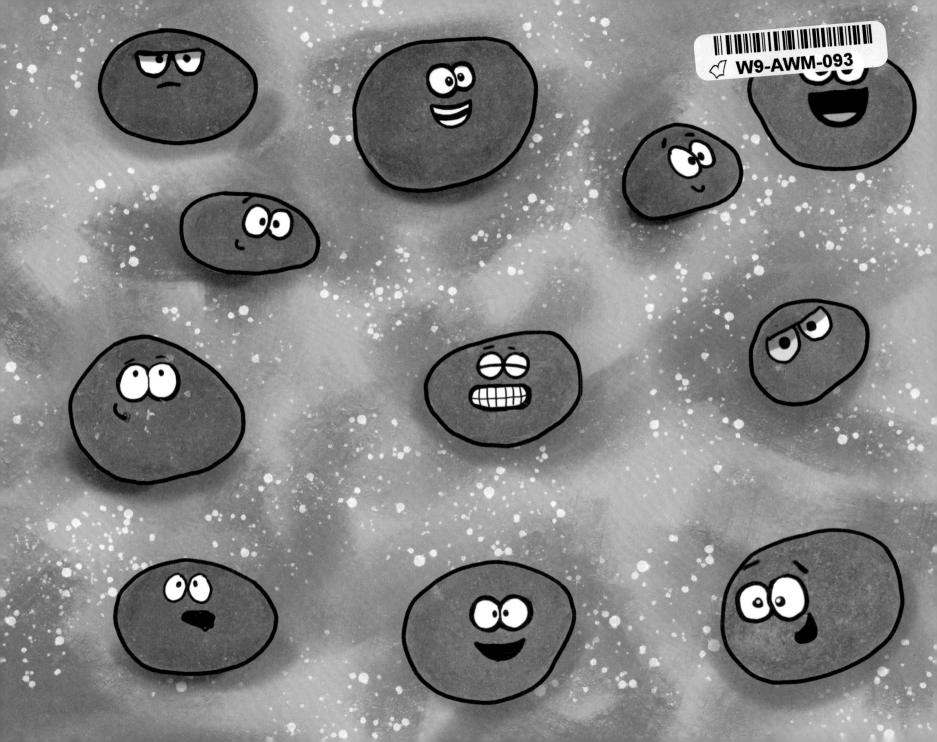

This book belongs to:

_____

_____

_____

# To my children Ryan and Anna.

Who love to play with a giant stone pile in the backyard,
which inevitably inspired this story.

This story is about one happy stone,
who was gray and round and rarely alone.
He lived with the others, all stacked in a pile,
and waited calmly with a large, friendly smile.

Each stone had a purpose, but it wasn't known yet.

Some would be **landscaping,**

and some a stone **pet.**

There were so many things that the stones could be.
The hardest part was just waiting to see.

Stone knew that his purpose would brighten someone's day,
He just wasn't sure how, or in what kind of way.
He imagined the things that he might soon become,
as he watched all the stones get picked one by one.

But his happy face slowly turned to a frown
as he watched the tall pile start to dwindle on down,
and although he was worried, he tried not to care
until it was clear--he was the last one there.

Then it finally happened. Stone was quickly picked up!
He was placed on a desk next to a very large cup.

As Stone looked around, he thought, "This is so great!"

But he soon discovered...he was a **dull paperweight.**

"I'm supposed to bring happiness, not hold paper still.
There must be a mistake. This just can't be my skill."

Then all of a sudden, a splatter flew high,
and then some bright scribbles came wiggling by.

They were headed right toward the short paper stack
and they filled up the paper on the front and the back.

They were all making art, it was happening so fast!
Stone feared that the paper would simply not last.

He couldn't believe just how much the pile grew.
Then he heard a small cry from the fun splatter crew,

"We knew that this pile was getting too tall!
There is no more paper! We have used it all!"
The scribbles all cried...They now saw it, too.
"This is a disaster. Oh, what will we do?"

Stone didn't want the scribbles to cry,
so he thought of something that they all could try.

He slowly rolled down the very large pile,
And said, "I know how to make you all smile!
I know I'm not paper, but I like art, too.
Do you think you could spare some red, yellow, and blue?"

They loved the idea and could not wait to start.
Scribble began making a happiness heart.
Splatter then painted some pale baby blue.
Another scribble added a sunny gold hue.

It didn't take long before more stones showed up,
and soon the line grew behind the large red cup.

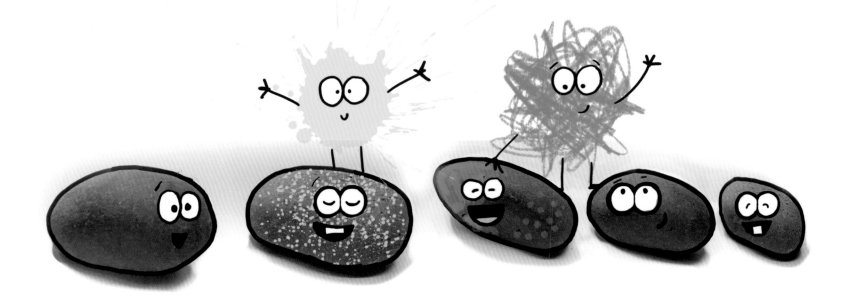

To Stone's surpise, he was picked up once more.
He had never heard of this happening before.

More art was added and he was on his way
to become a small gift to brighten someone's day.

Nearby, another stone's journey had begun.
He was spreading such happiness and having great fun!

Every time he **traveled**, someone **added their part,**
sometimes just a scribble, sometimes fancy art.

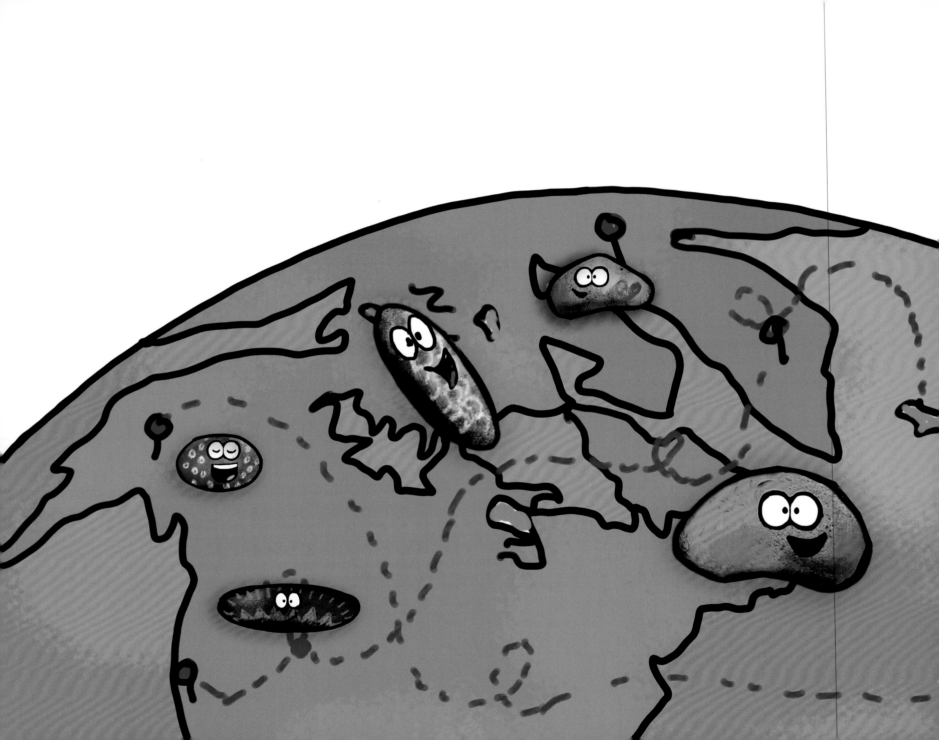

With each new layer, there was a story to share,
and soon scribble stones were seen everywhere.
They traveled the planet-- It was quite an event.
Bringing **happiness** and **fun** wherever they went.

Now thousands of stones inspire **creativity** each day.

All because of a paperweight with a will and a way!

# Scribble Stone Art Project

Scribble stones are intended to inspire creativity and spread happiness through collaborative art.

## HOW IT WORKS:

Find a stone and add some art,
a scribble, a splatter, or a happiness heart.
Then give it away and let someone know
that this scribble stone makes happiness grow.
It's so very simple and easy to do.
Just add some more art and give it away, too!

Give away          Give away          Give away

For information on the best medium to use on stones, or for stickers and extra tips visit:
www.dianealber.com/scribblestones

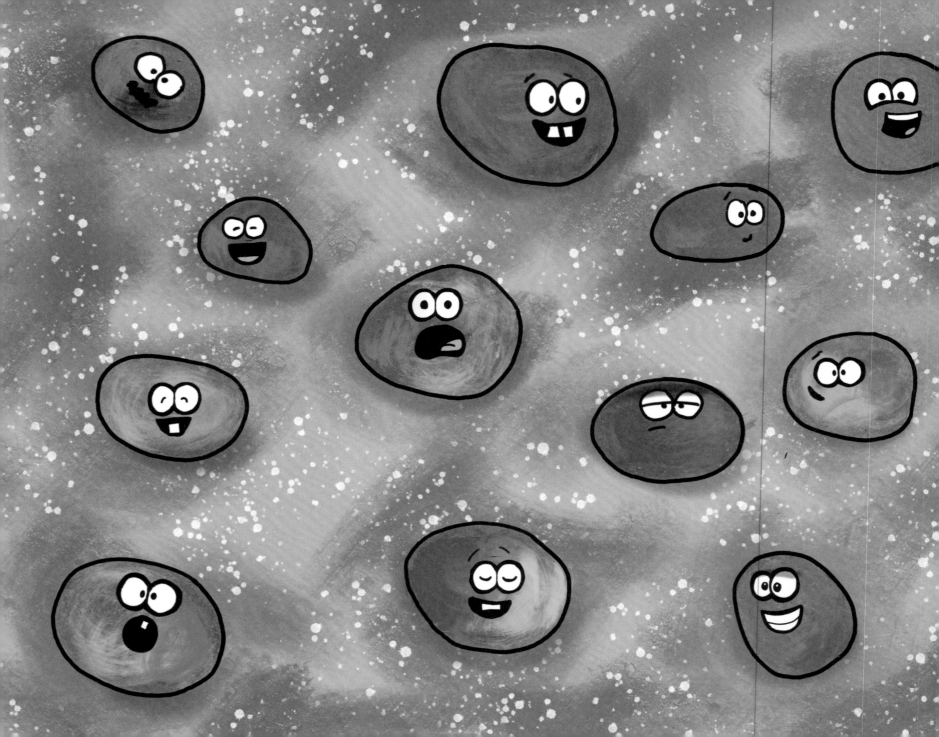